Written by Judith Koppens
Illustrated by Anouk Nijs

Mila
and the Monsters

Clavis

NEW YORK

My name is Mila.
Some days I live with my daddy
and some days I live with my mommy.
Today I'm staying at Mommy's.
Kitty is walking circles around me.
Hello Kitty, I'm so happy to see you too!

Mommy and I make dinner together.
I'm so good at helping Mommy.
Mommy cuts the vegetables and
I get to stir them in the pot.
Yummy, it smells delicious!

I can watch some television before I go to bed. I love to snuggle with Mommy on the couch.

There's a dog that makes funny jumps on the television. It makes Mommy and me laugh really hard. What a silly dog!

Then Mommy takes me to the bathroom.
I can climb the stairs all by myself,
but my monkey can't do it alone yet.

That's why I help him.
I go to the potty, wash my hands,
and brush my teeth.

I crawl in my warm bed.
Mommy reads me a bedtime story.
And then I close my eyes.

Tonight I'm going to dream about the silly dog on TV. Or about my monkey on the stairs. Or about Kitty making circles around me . . .

My bedroom at Mommy's is dark. Very dark . . .
And Mommy forgot to check if there are monsters.
Daddy always checks for monsters.
He looks everywhere . . . "No monsters here!"
Daddy says, sounding really tough.
"No horrible, smelly, hairy,
big, scary monsters here!"
"Mo-omy! You forgot to check
if there are any mo-onsters!"

"Oh, my dear Mila," Mommy says softly.
"Shall we look together then?"
Mommy looks behind the curtains first.
No monsters there.
No **tall** ones and no small ones . . .

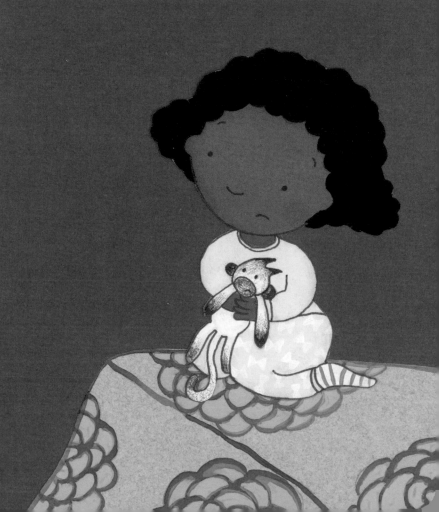

Then Mommy and I look
underneath the mat.
There are no monsters here
either. No **tall** ones and
no small ones, no **big** ones
and no thin ones . . .

"And don't forget the closet, Mommy. There are often horrible monsters hidden in the closet." But in the closet there are no monsters either.

No **tall** ones and no small ones, no **big** ones and no thin ones, no naughty ones and no sweet ones . . .

"There are no monsters here,"
Mommy says softly.
"Do you know why there are
never any monsters here?
No tall ones and no small ones,
no **big** ones and no thin ones, and not
even any naughty ones or sweet ones.
You know why, don't you?"

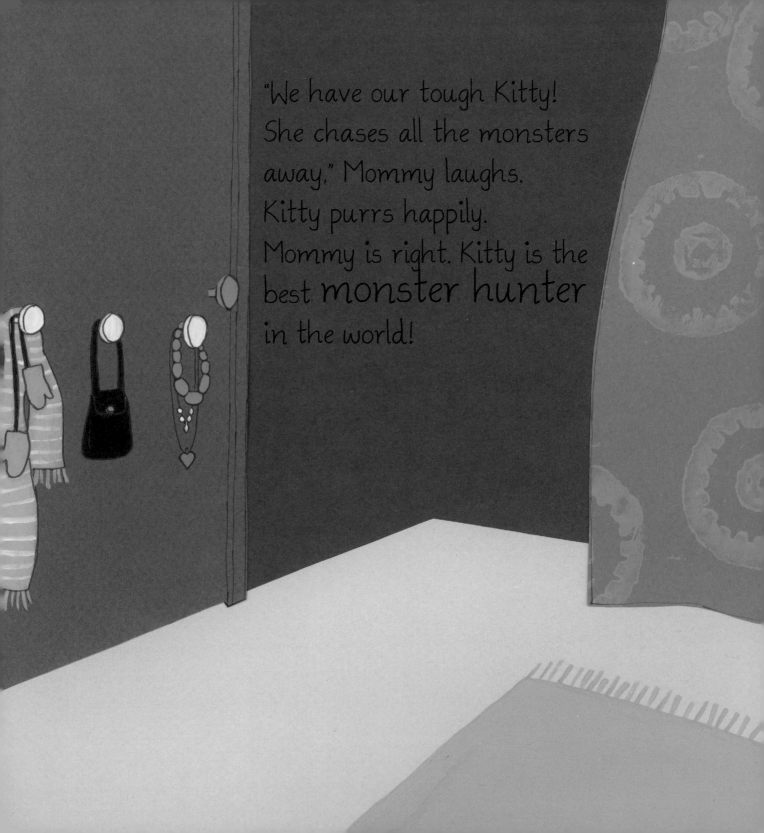

"We have our tough Kitty!
She chases all the monsters
away," Mommy laughs.
Kitty purrs happily.
Mommy is right. Kitty is the
best monster hunter
in the world!

Come, Kitty, you can stay with Mila tonight.
Sweet dreams, dear Mila!

ZZZZ

MEOW!